The Lion and the Bull

and other Aesop's Fables

Compiled by Vic Parker

Miles Kelly

First published in 2013 by Miles Kelly Publishing Ltd
Harding's Barn, Bardfield End Green, Thaxted, Essex, CM6 3PX, UK

2 4 6 8 10 9 7 5 3 1

Publishing Director Belinda Gallagher
Creative Director Jo Cowan
Editorial Director Rosie McGuire
Designer Joe Jones
Production Manager Elizabeth Collins
Reprographics Stephan Davis, Jennifer Hunt, Thom Allaway

ISBN 978-1-84810-939-1

Printed in China

British Library Cataloguing-in-Publication Data
A catalogue record for this book is available from the British Library

ACKNOWLEDGMENTS
The publishers would like to thank the following artists who have contributed to this book:
Cover: Frank Endersby
Advocate Art: Natalie Hinrichsen, Tamsin Hinrichsen
The Bright Agency: Marcin Piwowarski
Frank Endersby
Marco Furlotti
Jan Lewis (decorative frames)

Made with paper from a sustainable forest

www.mileskelly.net   info@mileskelly.net

www.factsforprojects.com

Contents

The Ant and the Dove

Once upon a time, a thirsty ant went to the stream for a drink. However, as the ant reached down to take a sip, it fell in, and was carried away by the rushing water.

The poor little ant was on the point of drowning when a dove, sitting on a tree overhanging the water, plucked a leaf and let it fall into the stream. The ant used the last of its strength to scramble on to it, then floated safely to the bank, exhausted but alive.

Soon afterwards, a bird-catcher came along

and saw the dove sitting in the tree. Unnoticed by the dove, he set a trap for her. But the ant saw what he had done. It raced up to the bird-catcher and bit him as hard as it could. The bird-catcher cried out, and the noise startled the dove, who flew off, safe and free.

The grateful heart will always find opportunities to show its gratitude.

5

The Wolf and the Shepherd

A shepherd was out on the hillside one day when he heard a yelping noise like a puppy. He was surprised to find a tiny wolf cub. The shepherd could not think of leaving the tiny creature there, so he took it home.

The shepherd reared the cub with his dogs, training it to herd the sheep this way and that. When

the cub grew to his full size, if ever a wolf stole a sheep from the flock, it would join the dogs in hunting it down. If the dogs failed to find the thief, the wolf would continue the hunt alone, and when it found the culprit, would stop and share the feast. As well as this, if some time passed without a sheep being carried off by the wolves, it would steal one itself.

Eventually, the shepherd became suspicious. So he kept a close watch on the wolf, until he caught it in the act of stealing a sheep. And that was the end of the ungrateful creature.

What's bred in the bone is sure to come out in the flesh.

The Woodman and the Serpent

Once upon a time, there was a woodman who had been hard at work all day, chopping logs in the snow. At last it was time to go home.

As he tramped through the forest, he noticed something black lying on the ground ahead. When he came closer, he saw that it was a serpent. It looked frozen with cold. The woodman took pity on the creature, and just in case there was some hope of reviving it, he picked it up and put it in his jacket to warm it.

As soon as the woodman got indoors he put

the serpent down before the fire. His children were curious and kept close watch. To their surprise, they suddenly saw the serpent's tail twitch. Its eyes opened. Then it wriggled. Then it flicked out its forked tongue. The children were delighted and one of them tried to stroke it. But the serpent raised its head and went to bite the child. Just in time, the woodman seized his axe and with one stroke cut the serpent in two.

Don't expect gratitude from the wicked.

The Wolf and the Crane

There was **once a hungry wolf** who was out hunting. He killed a young deer and began feasting on it, delighted with his meal.

Suddenly, he felt a small bone stick in his throat. He tried swallowing hard, but it wouldn't go down. Then he coughed, but the bone wouldn't come up. His throat was growing sore and he was getting agitated.

Desperately, the wolf begged other animals to try to remove the bone. "I would give anything," he gasped. But of course most

creatures would have nothing to do with him.

At last the crane agreed to try, and the wolf opened his jaws wide. Then, trying not to think of the sharp teeth, the crane put her long neck down the wolf's throat, and pulled the bone out with her beak. The wolf leapt about for joy.

"May I have the reward you promised?" asked the crane.

"You have put your head inside a wolf's mouth and taken it out again," said the wolf. "That should be reward enough."

Gratitude and greed do not go together.

The Old Hound

There was once a hound that had served its master well for many years. When they had been out hunting together, the hunt had been plentiful every time. However, now the hound was growing old and it had begun to lose its strength and speed, as well as most of its teeth.

One day, when out hunting, the hound's master startled a wild boar.

12

The boar set off at a pace and the man set the hound after it. The hound ran as fast as it could and caught up with the boar, and seized it by the ear. But as the hound had hardly any teeth, it could not keep a grip.
The boar managed to wrench free and escape.

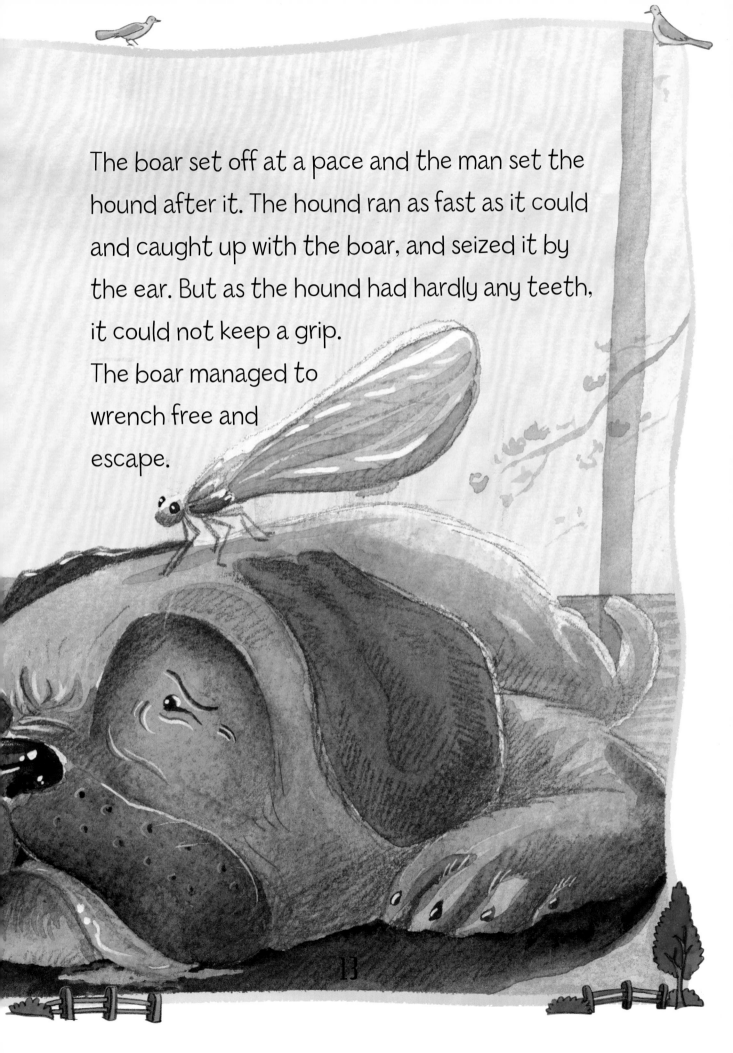

13

The man began to scold his dog, but the hound interrupted him with these words, "My will is as strong as ever, but my body is old and feeble. You ought to respect me for what I have been instead of abusing me for what I am now."

Respect your elders.

The Blind Man and the Cub

There was **once a blind man** who had so fine a sense of touch that when any animal was put into his hands, he could tell exactly what it was merely by feeling it. He could tell a mole from its velvety coat. He could tell a lizard from its scaly skin. He could tell a chick from its fluffy down and a goose from its long feathers.

One day, a wolf cub was placed in his hands, and he was asked what he thought it was. He felt the cub all over for some time, and then said, "Indeed, I am not sure whether it is a wolf's cub

or a fox's, but this I do know – it would never do to trust it in a herd of sheep."

Evil tendencies are early shown.

The Quack Frog

Once upon a time, a frog lived deep in the marshes, where no one ever came to see him. He felt unloved and quite alone. 'How can I make myself important to others,' he wondered, 'so that they want to see me and talk to me?'

The frog thought hard and hit upon an idea. He dressed himself as a doctor and practiced putting on a wise expression, and talking in a clever way. Then he left his home in the marshes and went off into the world, proclaiming to be a learned doctor, knowledgeable about medicines and able to cure diseases.

Creatures came from far and wide to see if he could cure their illnesses. But among the crowd was a fox, who called out, "You, a doctor! How can you claim to heal others when you cannot even cure your own bent legs and blotched and wrinkled skin?"

Those who say they can heal others should first heal themselves, then they may be believed.

18

The Lion
and the
Bull

A long time ago, a bull lived among a herd of cattle in a field of lush grass. He grew fat through grazing and living an easy life.

One day a lion passed by the field. When he saw the cattle his mouth began to water – but when he spied the huge bull he began to drool. The lion went away and thought hard about how he could get the bull in his clutches.

After a while he hit upon an idea, and sent the bull an invitation to come to dinner. The bull was flattered at being asked to dine with the

King of the Beasts and of course he accepted at once. He boasted to all the cattle in the field about his important appointment and made sure that his coat was free of mud and his hooves and horns were shining.

That evening, at the appointed hour, the excited bull made his way to the lion's den. The lion welcomed him and told the bull to come in and make himself at home. However, the bull noticed that although he saw a

great array of saucepans, roasting spits and other kitchen equipment, there was little sign of anything cooking other than soup.

The bull was clever and his suspicions were immediately aroused. So he turned on his heels and walked out.

21

The lion called after him in a hurt tone to ask the reason why, and the bull turned around and said, "I have reason enough. When I saw all your preparations it struck me at once that dinner was to be a bull."

If you lay your plans in front of your enemies you will fail.

Androcles
and the
Lion

In ancient days long gone by, there was once a slave named Androcles who was forced to work under a very cruel master. One day he took his chance and managed to escape from his master's house, fleeing to the surrounding forest. Androcles was of course overjoyed to be free, but now he had new troubles. What was he to do next? Where was he to go? How was he to live?

He wandered through the forest, pondering these questions, when he came upon a mighty lion groaning with pain. Androcles' first thought

was to run for his life. But then he stood, curious as to why the lion didn't spring up and pounce. After a while, when the lion had continued to groan, but not move at all, Androcles cautiously went closer... and closer... and closer... until he was near enough to touch the lion.

Then the great beast stretched out its paw, and Androcles saw that it was swollen and bleeding. Full of pity, and forgetting his fear, he bent to examine it. He discovered that a huge thorn was stuck in it, which was causing the pain. He 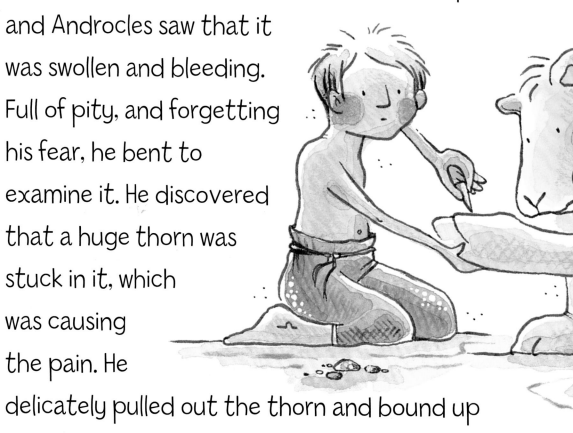 delicately pulled out the thorn and bound up the lion's paw. The lion bowed its mighty head to

Androcles and rubbed its mane against him, and even licked his hand.

Androcles followed the lion to its cave and took shelter there. The great beast then bounded off to hunt for meat for Androcles to eat, and this is how they lived from then on – until one day, when hunters came to that part of the forest. Androcles and the lion tried to flee, but they were outnumbered and the hunters caught them, and dragged them both off to the city. The lion was taken away to fight in front of huge crowds at the arena, for in those days people thought it was sport to see men and animals fight to the death.

Meanwhile, Androcles was put on trial for escaping from his master's house. His punishment was death – by being thrown to a lion

in the arena.

The day arrived when fighting in the arena was to take place. Everyone in the city came to see the spectacle, ruled over by the emperor and his court. After several men had fought each other before the roaring crowd, Androcles was led out to the center of the sandy arena. He stood in terror, fearing the worst. Then a lion was let loose from a dungeon beneath the arena and came bounding towards Androcles.

But as soon as the lion came near to Androcles it stopped and bowed its head, licking his hands. It was the lion from the forest – Androcles' friend.

Everyone was astounded, and the emperor summoned Androcles to him, who told the whole story. After hearing this, the emperor told Androcles that he was pardoned and free to go,

and the lion was also let loose to return to its home in the forest.

Gratitude is the sign of noble souls.

The Nurse and the Wolf

There was once a nurse who was looking after a little child who kept crying. "Be quiet now," she said, holding the child, "if you make that noise again I will give you to the wolf."

Now it happened that a wolf was passing under the window and heard the nurse say this. So he crouched down by the house and waited.

'I am in luck today,' he thought. 'The child is sure to cry again soon, then the nurse will throw it out for me to grab. And a daintier morsel I haven't had for many a day.'

So the wolf waited and waited, until at last he heard the child crying again. The wolf sat under the window and looked up to the nurse, wagging his tail. But all the nurse did was gasp in horror and slam the window shut. She shrieked, calling for help, and the dogs of the house came bounding out, snarling.

Then the wolf realized that the nurse hadn't meant what she said, and he fled for his life, his tail between his legs.

Enemies' promises were made to be broken.

The Soldier
and his
Horse

It was wartime, and a soldier looked after his horse with great care. He gave it a plentiful supply of oats and water, and groomed and exercised it every day, for he wished the horse to be strong enough to endure the hardships of the battlefield.

However when the war was over, the soldier completely changed his

habits. He made the horse do all sorts of hard tasks, such as drawing carts and carrying heavy packs. He gave it only chaff to eat and hardly ever brushed its coat or checked its hooves.

The time came when war broke out again. Once more, the soldier saddled his horse for battle. He put on his heavy uniform along with his pack and weapons, then mounted his horse. But the poor horse sank under his weight.

"You will have to go to battle on foot," said the horse. "Due to hard work and bad food, you have turned me into a donkey, and you cannot in a moment turn me into a horse again."

When you have something that is of value, always look after it properly.

The Wolves and the Dogs

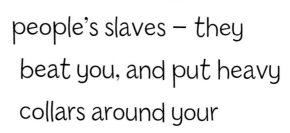

Once upon a time, the wolves said to the dogs, "Why should we continue to be enemies any longer? You are like us in many ways, the main difference between us is only that of training. We live a life of freedom, but you are people's slaves – they beat you, and put heavy collars around your

necks, and make you keep watch over their flocks and herds. To top it off, they give you nothing but bones to eat." The dogs hung their heads in shame and mumbled in agreement.

The wolves continued, "We don't think you should put up with it any longer. Hand over the flocks to us, and we will all live on the fat of the land and feast together."

The dogs thought this sounded like a good plan. The wolves' clever words had persuaded them, and they went off with the wolves to their den. But no sooner were they inside than the wolves set upon them and tore them to pieces.

Traitors richly deserve their fate.

The Donkey and the Wolf

There was **once a donkey** who was feeding in a meadow. To his horror, he caught sight of his enemy the wolf approaching in the distance, and knew he would be eaten unless he came up with a plan. So the donkey suddenly pretended to be very lame and hobbled painfully along. When the wolf reached him, he asked the donkey how he came to be so lame.

"I went through a hedge and stepped on a thorn," said the donkey. "Please would you pull the offending thorn out with your teeth dear

wolf? Just in case, when you eat me, it should stick in your throat and hurt you very much."

"How thoughtful of you," snarled the wolf, and said that of course he would help. He told the donkey to lift up his foot, and set his mind to getting out the thorn.

But the donkey suddenly kicked out with his heels and gave the wolf a blow to the mouth, breaking

his teeth. He then galloped off at full speed.

As soon as he was able, the wolf growled to himself, "It serves me right. My father taught me to kill, and I should have stuck to that trade instead of attempting to cure."

Everyone has his trade and should stick to it.

The Athenian and the Theban

A man from the city of Athens and a man from the city of Thebes were once traveling together. They passed the time in conversation, as is the way of travelers. After discussing a variety of subjects they began to talk about the heroes of old – mighty men who were half-gods, who had performed incredible feats of strength and bravery. Each traveler was full of praise for the heroes of his own city.

Eventually, the man from Thebes claimed that the famous Hercules was the greatest hero

who had ever lived on Earth, and now occupied a foremost place among the gods. Hercules was a mighty warrior who had killed an enormous lion, beaten a many-headed dragon, captured a giant bull, and stolen a three-headed dog that guarded the gates of hell, among other feats.

At this, the man from Athens insisted that the hero Theseus was far superior, and began to explain why. Theseus, he said, was more intelligent than Hercules. After all, he had used his wits to enter a complicated underground maze called a labyrinth and slay a bull-headed monster called the Minotaur that lived there.

The man from Athens was very good at arguing, and as the man from Thebes was no match for him, he eventually had to give in. "All right, have it your way," he cried. "I only hope that when our heroes are angry with us, Athens

may suffer from the fury of Hercules, and Thebes from the wrath of Theseus."

Brains may beat brawn.

The Cat and the Birds

A cat once heard that the birds in a nearby aviary had fallen ill. He thought this would be an ideal time to catch them. So disguised as a doctor, the cat set off for the aviary.

Once there, the cat knocked at the door, and enquired after the birds' health.

"We shall be much better," they replied, without letting him in, "when we have seen the last of you."

A villain may disguise himself, but he will not deceive the wise.

40